S0-AYP-267

This

Matzah Ball Book

belongs to:

_____

_____

_____

Klutzy   Shmutzy

Kvetchy   Shluffy   Noshy

Shluffy Girl
Copyright © 2005 by Anne-Marie Asner
Second Printing March 2006
Printed in the United States of America
All rights reserved
www.matzahballbooks.com
Library of Congress Control Number: 2005922188
ISBN-13: 978-0-9753629-2-1
ISBN-10: 0-9753629-2-5

Shluffy Girl

by Anne-Marie Baila Asner

MATZAH BALL BOOKS

Nap time is Shluffy Girl's favorite time of the day.

But for Shluffy Girl, nap time is almost all the time.

Eating, reading and playing don't stop Shluffy Girl from taking a snooze. She can sleep pretty much anywhere and anytime.

Shluffy Girl's favorite thing to do is to have slumber parties with her friends.

Last weekend, Shluffy Girl invited Kibbitzy Girl and Shmutzy Girl to sleep over.

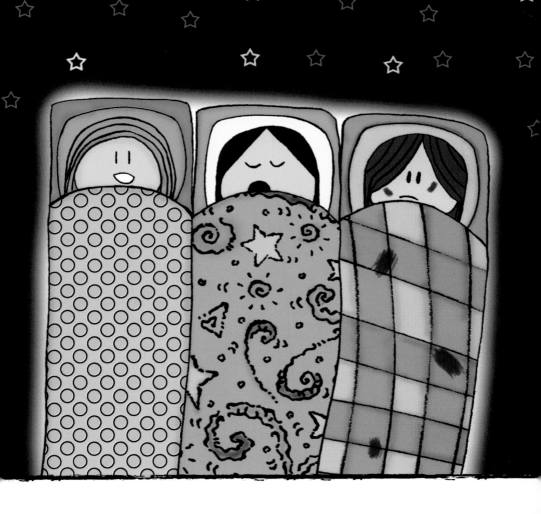

Kibbitzy Girl, who loves to joke around, kept
Shmutzy Girl awake most of the night. But
Shluffy Girl managed to fall asleep just fine.

Sometimes Shluffy Girl's love for sleep gets her into trouble.

When she naps on the bus, Shluffy Girl misses her stop. "Uh oh," said Shluffy Girl when she woke up. "It's a long walk home from here."

When she falls asleep in class, Shluffy Girl gets scolded. "Shluffy Girl! How can you learn when you're always sleeping?" asked her teacher.

When she shluffs during recess, sometimes
Shluffy Girl gets hurt. "Ow!" she cried as Klutzy Boy
tripped over her.

"Oops, I should have looked," said Klutzy Boy.
"But people usually aren't sleeping in the middle of
the playground."

Shluffy Girl's biggest problem is her good friend
Kvetchy Boy.

Kvetchy Boy always complains about how much
Shluffy Girl sleeps.

"Sleep, sleep, sleep. All you do is sleep,"
said Kvetchy Boy.

"Why does it bother you so much that I love to sleep? Why do you always complain about it?" asked Shluffy Girl.

"Shluffy Girl, you're not fun to hang out with because you're always sleeping. You even fell asleep at my birthday party," said Kvetchy Boy.

"I'm sorry, Kvetchy Boy," said Shluffy Girl. "I didn't mean to hurt your feelings."

"It's not just that," said Kvetchy Boy. "I'm a little worried. I don't know anyone, other than my bubbe and zaide, who sleeps so much."

The next day, Shluffy Girl's mother took her to
the doctor to make sure nothing was the matter.

"Everything seems to be all right," said the doctor. "Maybe Shluffy Girl is growing and needs extra rest or maybe she just likes to sleep."

"But this much sleep? She sleeps all the time," said Shluffy Girl's mom.

"Well, there's a time and place for most everything. Maybe Shluffy Girl could try sleeping only when she's really tired. Probably nap time and night time are enough."

With a lot of effort, Shluffy Girl stopped napping on the bus and she no longer misses her stop.

She stopped sleeping in class and she learns
a lot more.

And she stopped sleeping during recess and she no longer gets hurt.

Now, Shluffy Girl saves her naps for nap time.

Shluffy Girl still loves to sleep and can't wait until her next slumber party.

And Shluffy Girl is happiest of all when each day comes to an end and she finally can snuggle under the covers, turn out the light and say, "Good night."

Kvetchy   Shluffy   Noshy

Klutzy　　Shmutzy

Glossary

A Bissle (little bit) of Yiddish

Bubbe (bŭ-bē) *n.* grandmother

Keppy (kĕpp-ē) *n.* head; *adj.* smart, using one's head

Kibbitzy (kĭbbĭtz-ē) *v. kibbitz* to joke around; *adj. kibbitzy*

Klutzy (klŭts-ē) *adj.* clumsy

Kvelly (k'vĕll-ē) *v. kvell* to be proud, pleased; *adj. kvelly*

Kvetchy (k'vĕtch-ē) *adj.* whiny, complaining

Noshy (nŏsh-ē) *v. nosh* to snack; *adj. noshy*

Shayna Punim (shā-nă pŭ-nĭm) *adj.* pretty *(shayna)*; *n.* face *(punim)*

Shleppy (shlĕp-ē) *v. shlep* to carry or drag; *adj. shleppy*

Shluffy (shlŭf-ē) *adj.* sleepy, tired

Shmoozy (shmooz-ē) *adj.* chatty, friendly

Shmutzy (shmŭtz-ē) *adj.* dirty, messy

Tushy (tŭsh-ē) *n.* buttocks, bottom

Zaide (zā-dē) *n.* grandfather